For my dear hat-wearing sister, Jessie

First U.S. edition 2014

Library of Congress Catalog Card Number 2013955693

ISBN 978-0-7636-7406-9

14 15 16 17 18 19 TLF 10 9 8 7 6 5 4 3 2 1

Printed in Dongguan, Guangdong, China

This book was typeset in Stempel Schneidler.
The illustrations were done in mixed media.

TEMPLAR BOOKS

an imprint of Candlewick Press

99 Dover Street

Somerville, Massachusetts 02144

www.candlewick.com

OLIVE
AND THE
EMBARRASSING
GIFT

TOR FREEMAN

templar books
an imprint of Candlewick Press

Joe gave Olive a gift.

"They're matching hats!" said Joe. "And they say BEST FRIENDS on them, because that's what we are."

"Oh, yes," said Olive. "Thank you, Joe."

Olive and Joe saw
Ziggy on his skateboard.
"Hi, Ziggy!" said Joe.

"Ha!" said Ziggy.

"I'm not sure it's quite hat weather today," said Olive.

"Well, it's not really that sort of hat," said Joe. "It's more of an everyday hat!"

"I suppose so," said Olive.

Olive and Joe
saw Lola in the park.
"Hi, Lola," said Joe.

"Hee, hee,"
said Lola.

"Maybe I should take off
my hat so I don't lose it,"
said Olive.
"It's a little big."

"It's OK," said Joe.
"These hats are so stretchy
they won't ever fall off!"

"Great," said Olive.

Joe stopped to sniff some flowers.
Matt was nearby, working on a painting.

"Ha, ha!" said Matt.
"Boy, Olive, you look silly in that hat!"

Olive's tummy felt funny, so she went to sit by herself for a moment.

How lovely and peaceful it was.

"Olive!" said Molly.
"What HAVE you got
on your head?"

"I'm not Olive," said Olive.

Olive just wanted to be alone.
But she could hear
someone else coming!

Olive couldn't take it any longer.
She had to do something.

"Don't you like your hat?" asked Joe.

said Olive.

But it was too late.

Joe had left. Oh, dear.
Olive had NOT been a good friend.

She had to make it up to Joe.

Olive went into the store on the corner.

Five minutes later, she came out again.

Olive looked really silly now.

Olive stood on the sidewalk.

Lola and

Molly and

Ziggy and

Matt

saw Olive.

"Ha, ha, ha!" they said.

"What?" said Olive.

OLIVE AND JOE ARE BEST FRIENDS

BEST FRIENDS

Then along came Joe.

"What are you doing, Olive?"
he asked.

"I am wearing my favorite hat and my new sign," said Olive. "The sign says OLIVE AND JOE ARE BEST FRIENDS . . ."

"because that's what we *are*."